Rules for ruined cities, their monsters and custom Beastfolk, for level 1+

Written and laid out by Erick N. Bouchard

Art by Alexey Aparin (pocketlands.com)

Cover and *Four Against Darkness* game by Andrea Sfiligoi

Feedback by Daniel Casquilho. Proofreading by Alun Heseltine.

Borders by Ulysse Bouchard. Icons by game-icons.net

Requires *Four Against Darkness*. Customized classes require *Four Against the Abyss*.

The *Bestiary Card Deck* is optional and available at pocketlands.com

For more about Norindaal, the setting for *Four Against Darkness*:

https://sites.google.com/site/norindaal/

Buy PDFs on www.ganeshagames.net

Buy books on www.lulu.com/spotlight/songofblades

Contents

Introduction

This book showcases the unique monsters from Alexey Aparin's Bestiary Card Deck. These critters, also featured in Tome 2 of *Treacheries of the Troublesome Towns*, are provided here with rules to use them outside the context of towns.

In this book you will also find:

- Rules to generate Ruined Cities;
- New tables for special features, treasure and magic;
- Rules for creating your own classes of beastfolk characters;
- New spells to be used in game-mastered games with the "RPG-Lite Option" in the 4AD book.

Note: Treacheries of the Troublesome (TTT) is not published yet at the time of this writing. When these monsters will appear in TTT, their profiles will be adjusted for play in towns and based on the party's highest character level. TTT is designed for advanced play and features more sophisticated rules intended for experienced players.

Players who prefer the simpler play style outlined in *Four Against Darkness* will enjoy this book's more direct "kill and loot" approach.

Scaling Up With Party Level

(Optional Rules)

The foe profiles assume that, at the adventure's start, your highest character level is 1. If this isn't the case, to keep the game challenging, for each level above 1 your highest level character has, either:

- Increase the number of Vermin and Minions by 2;
- Increase the level and life of Bosses and Weird Monsters by 1.
- At Expert tier or above, Vermin will count as Minions for XP purposes.

Customization

As with everything in *Four Against Darkness*, every rule in this book is optional. What is "official" is what you decide it to be. You, as the "Play Master", are both the player and referee. Use only the rules you like, change them or write new ones. You're not cheating if you're having fun.

Custom Classes

Create Your Own Beastfolk Class!

Anything you can imagine, however strange or amazing, surely has its likeness on Norindaal, for the gods show unbridled imagination as their Godgame unfolds onto the world. Whereas the 4AD books provide you with many classes to represent the manifold species of beastfolk, no doubt your imagination can envision many more.

These rules allow you to mix and match features to create new and unique classes, roughly equivalent in

terms of power to those from *Four Against Darkness*. These classes are meant to represent beastfolk not otherwise covered in this book or another. If a class already exists, use the "official" one instead!

To build a custom class, pick up to 4 Major Traits from the list below. A Major Trait can be traded for 2 Minor Traits. If you wish, you can also take up to 2 Restrictions: each Restriction gives you one additional Minor Trait. You cannot use Restrictions to acquire Major Traits.

Default Profile

The default "free" profile for beastfolk, without any Major or Minor Trait added, is the following:

Traits: No bonus to either Attack or Defense.

Saves: Like barbarians.

Armor allowed: None.

Weapons allowed: Light weapons only.

Starting equipment: One of weapon among those allowed, one choice of armor among those allowed.

Starting wealth: 2d6 gp.

Life: 3+L. A L1 character with this generic class profile has 4 life.

Expert skills: For games above L5, by default beast folk characters of Expert levels use the swashbucklers' list (4AA). See *Four Against the Abyss* for rules about characters of L6-9 and *Four Against the Forsaken Depths* for higher levels.

Conditions

The maximum total bonus to both Attack and Defense is the character's level (L). A class built with the present system can therefore have either Primary Attack (+L to Attack) OR Primary Defense (+L to Defense), but not both, nor is it possible to have Primary Attack and Secondary Defense or the other way around. However, having both Secondary Attack and Secondary Defense is allowed.

Avoid making overpowered classes. While the Traits offered shouldn't make the 4AD classes obsolete, open systems are open to abuse. Don't spoil your own fun!

Major Trait List

Innate Expert Skill: This Trait can be taken only once. Your class starts with 1 Expert skill at L1 from *Four Against the Abyss* among the following: Acute Hearing, Arcane Tanner, Combat Acrobatics, Continual Light, Commanding Presence, Deadly Accuracy (choose one ranged weapon), Dead Shot, Deadly Strike, Detective, Dying Action, Gladiator, Impervious, Intuition, Knife Throwing, Negotiator, Poison Resistance, Quick Footed, Spore Alchemy, Spot Weakness, Strong Will, Super Logic, Sworn Enemy, Terrifying Savagery, Withstand Pain.

Primary Attack: You add the character's full level to all Attack rolls.

Primary Defense: You add the character's full level to Defense rolls.

Primary Armor Proficiency: Your class can use heavy armor, light armor and shields.

Primary Natural Weapon: Your class' unarmed attacks counts as two-handed weapons (choose either crushing or slashing). This class cannot use a shield when performing a Primary Natural Attack.

Primary Weapon Proficiency: Your class can use all weapons, melee and ranged, excluding technological weapons like firearms and clockwork chainsaws.

Primary Stamina: Your class' starting life is 6+L (7 life at L1).

Spellcasting: Your class can cast 1 spell per level, like elves and with the same restrictions. If only one spell can be cast, your class gets 1 additional use per game. No spells beyond the 6 basic spells in 4AD can be learned UNLESS you choose to give your class access to one, and only one, spell from another book. This spell cannot be of Expert level or higher and normal components are required.

In all cases, the class does not use a spellbook and cannot learn new spells with scrolls or as skills. This Trait cannot be taken if your class also has Primary Defense. This Trait can be taken only once.

Wings: Your class can fly and carry another character of the same size or lesser when doing so. This cannot be done when wearing armor. If carrying anyone, the flyer cannot Attack in combat and suffers a -1 penalty to Defense. Outdoors, flying characters can move at thrice the usual walking speed over long ranges, but at the risk of getting separated from the party.

Minor Traits List

Alternate Save: You may choose another class "to save as" among those from 4AD (barbarian, elf, warrior, etc.). This also changes the Expert skills allowed to your class to the one it "saves as". This does not give your class other class-specific abilities, such as the ability to pick locks or disarm traps, nor does it give non-spellcasters access to spell-related skills (e.g. Scroll Maker), skills that require specific class abilities (e.g. Berserk Fury).

Amphibious: You breathe underwater. Swimming saves are always successful.

Hated Foe: If your class has Primary Attack, it also gets a +1 Attack bonus versus a specific monster type (e.g. undead, orcs, demons, rat monsters, plant monsters, etc.) If your class has Secondary Attack, this bonus increases to +L instead of +½L. If your class has neither Primary nor Secondary Attack, this bonus is +½L. However, this monster type will hate your class.

Night Vision: Your class needs no lantern and sees perfectly in the dark.

Ranged Fighter: Your class can use ranged weapons like bows and slings, except technological ones like firearms, adding +L to ranged Attacks.

Secondary Attack: You add +½L to melee Attack rolls.

Secondary Defense: You add +½L to Defense rolls.

Secondary Armor Proficiency: You can use light armor OR shields. Decide which at class creation.

Secondary Weapon Proficiency: You can use all one-handed melee weapons, excluding technological weapons like clockwork chainsaws.

Secondary Natural Weapon: Your unarmed attacks count as light weapons (choose crushing or slashing). This is similar to the Brawler skill from 4AA, and does not stack.

Secondary Stamina: Your starting life is 4+L (5 life at L1).

Specialized Save: In addition to basic class bonuses, you get to add +L to a specific save type (e.g. will, strength, puzzles, persuasion, stealth, etc.) This cannot confer the class abilities exclusive to another class, such as a rogue's trap disarming and lock picking abilities.

Supplemental Stamina: Increase your class' starting life by +1. This can be taken several times but cannot bring your class' life above 7+L (8 life at L1).

Woo: It works like satyrs (see TCOTFD)*.

Restrictions List

Restrictions are deliberately harsh, so you can't pick disadvantages that confer minimal nuisances. There are no "cosmetic limitations" you can take without a significant disadvantage.

Bloodthirsty: On Attack or Spellcasting rolls of 1, the class hits a random party member, automatically hitting for 1 Life damage. This applies to all Attack and Spellcasting rolls, including natural weapons and skills.

Feral: The class always attacks all monsters that have even the smallest odds of being hostile (never roll for reactions) and fights to the death in all combat situations, whatever the odds and the conditions, fighting alone if need be. Monsters or NPCs with absolutely no odds of being hostile are not attacked. (e.g. wandering alchemists).

Hated: Bosses and Weird Monsters direct all their attacks against this class.

Infected: The class always starts each adventure with the Dark Plague , but at full life points. Roll d8 for every room or corridor, on a 1 the character loses 1 life. This cannot be cured in any fashion.

Limited: Progress in levels beyond L3 cost 1 more XP roll (2 XP for L4+).

Magic Bane: You cannot use magic items or carry them, like barbarians.

Stupid*: Use Stupidity rules like green trolls (see Wayfarers & Adventurers).

Vampiric: For every 2 encounters that pass without a combat, characters of that class loses 1 life. This can't bring the beast folk character under 1 life.

***Extraneous Options:** These traits refer to books other than 4AD and 4AA. They're provided to widen your span of choices. Feel free to ignore them if you don't have these books.*

Sample Beastfolk

Cat Folk: Innate Expert Skill (Spot Weakness), Primary Attack, Secondary Armor Proficiency, Secondary Weapon Proficiency, Secondary Natural Weapon, Secondary Stamina.

Crocodile Folk: Amphibious, Feral, Innate Expert Skill (Terrifying Savagery), Primary Attack, Primary Natural Weapon, Primary Stamina, Secondary Weapon Proficiency, Stupid.

Hare Folk: Innate Expert Skill (Acute Hearing), Primary Weapon Proficiency, Secondary Armor Proficiency, Secondary Attack, Secondary Defense, Secondary Stamina.

Hound Folk: Innate Expert Skill (Detective), Magic Bane, Primary Attack, Primary Armor Proficiency, Secondary Weapon Proficiency, Primary Stamina.

Mouse Folk: Night Vision, Primary Defense, Ranged Fighter, Secondary Armor Proficiency, Secondary Stamina, Spellcasting (Escape only).

Mosquito Folk: Hated Foe (reptiles), Ranged Fighter, Secondary Attack, Secondary Defense, Secondary Armor Proficiency, Secondary Natural Weapon, Secondary Stamina, Vampiric, Wings.

Sheep Folk: Primary Stamina, Secondary Attack, Secondary Defense, Secondary Armor Proficiency, Secondary Weapon Proficiency, Spellcasting (Sleep only).

Spider Folk: Innate Expert Skill (Arcane Tanner), Hated, Primary Defense, Secondary Armor Proficiency, Secondary Weapon Proficiency, Secondary Natural Weapon, Primary Stamina.

Swine Folk: Bloodthirsty, Infected, Innate Expert Skill (Withstand Pain), Primary Attack, Primary Armor Proficiency, Primary Stamina, Primary Weapon Proficiency.

RPG Spells

These new spells, allowed to any spellcasting character of any level such as elves and wizards (but not clerics), are intended for players who use *Four Against Darkness* as a multiplayer roleplaying game under the guidance of a Game Master. These spells reveal secrets that will be hard to use in solo play and make sense only under the implicit social contract of trust that binds players and Game Master. Since these spells may affect things that the Game Master has decided or improvised, the way these spells work, and what they reveal, is to be interpreted in good faith. The spells effect should be useful considering that the players have had to renounce other spells for them. In other words, if you allow these spells and the casting of one of these reveals your well-crafted plans, don't cheat the players: reveal the truth and use the resulting consequences as a story hook for dramatic developments. Remember that the GM's role is never to push the players into following a pre-imagined story, but rather to throw challenges and choices at them, and generate the consequences, neither to reward or to punish the *players*, in order to make for an interesting game for everybody.

Only characters can cast these spells. NPCs and retainers cannot.

Dispel Illusion

This spell reveals the true nature of all beings in the area, whose true form is revealed for all to see. The illusion is broken. The GM must reveal to the players the true form of the entities hidden under a false appearance. This includes illusions, spells of invisibility, as well as any shape-changers like chest monsters, werewolves, doppelgängers, deities but not monsters which have human form, like vampires, unless they were in animal form (e.g. bat). The effect lasts for one encounter. Only the illusion is lifted; the beings' true intentions are not (but see Reveal intentions, below).

Omen

This spell reveals useful information about the greatest danger that the party is likely to encounter in the present game session, and ways to avoid or mitigate it. It could reveal who is a traitor and the nature of their forces (e.g. "the mastermind is a L9 chaos lord with armies of goat men and gutter elves"), but without evidence to convince the authorities to act. Only the caster is sure of the omen's truth. Outsiders cannot distinguish this spell from the lunatic ravings of the mad. In game terms, if the GM has no better idea to help the caster, this spell works like the "Secret of a Monster" from the 4AD book against the Final Boss, or any similar secret.

Reveal Intentions

This mind-reading spell reveals, in useful ways, the current intentions and motivations of a single target. This includes the target's next reaction (make a reaction roll ahead, if applicable). Detailed plans are not revealed, only general intent, both global and personal, including intent against the party. Examples:

"The lich is obsessed with knowledge of the Forbidden Depths and plans to rob the temple library, but she isn't hostile."

"The little boy is hungry and sees you as easy prey, but he'll be docile if fed."

"The succubus' invite is sincere but she's concerned about her mortgage. She will ask for hefty payment after her service."

"The orc hates you and wants you dead because your party killed his mother and siblings in the last dungeon you visited."

"The flamingo expects to be worshipped and finds your lack of faith disturbing."

"The merchant is a quadriloch in disguise and wants to sell you something cursed."

The spell cannot discern whether a being is "good" or "evil", because this is subjective (everybody thinks of themselves as "good"), but will clarify what the target intends to do.

The spell lasts for one entire encounter.

Ruined City Maps

The following rules allow you to generate maps and tables for Ruined Cities. If you prefer, use the dungeon rules from 4AD to draw the dungeon and the tables here for room content.

Drawing Ruin Maps

Long ago, this used to be a town or city, but the ravages of time has made it unpredictable and deadly.

Drawing the Rooms

Take a sheet of paper. Drop 10d6 (or 10d4 for fewer corridors) over it.

Draw a circle on the map around each die. Leave it there or remember the number of all dice dropped. You should normally get 10 circles. If 2 or more dice fell side by side (they touch), draw the circle around all of them and keep only the highest die inside that big circle. Don't "explode" those dice.

If any die falls off the map, don't use it. If the dice all fall off, start again. You need at least 1 die on your map. In the case of ties, choose or decide at random. Don't roll new dice on your map!

Drawing the Corridors

The room closest to the map's edge has a corridor that leads to an entrance or exit (which is the same thing) out of the ruins. When you exit the map, your adventure is over. Using a marker, draw a line from that room to represent a corridor that exits the map. It counts as a corridor for the purpose of a room's connections (see below).

Then, starting with the room that has the highest number, draw a number of lines that connect that room to another room, starting with the closest room. Those lines are corridors.

If you have too many corridors left for the number of rooms available, draw lines (corridors) leading outside the map. Ignore the leftovers.

All rooms must be connected together. If you don't have enough "corridors slots", add as much as needed. Make the additional connecting corridors as short as possible, by connecting the rooms closest to one another. In the end, it must be possible to move to each and any room from the entrance.

Dungeon Entrance

Draw stairs in the the room closest to the center of your Ruined City map. This is the entrance to an underground dungeon. You may explore it or not.

If you do, use *Four Against Darkness* or any dungeon supplement such as *Warlike Woes*, *Twisted Dungeons*, *Caverns of Chaos* or *Digressions of the Devouring Dead* to generate a "normal" dungeon.

Starting Room

Your party starts at the entrance/exit (the main one, or any one generated in the ruins generation process). You may likewise leave by any of them.

BLAZEDAWN

NOW THE FLOOD WEEPS O'ER THEIR HALLS

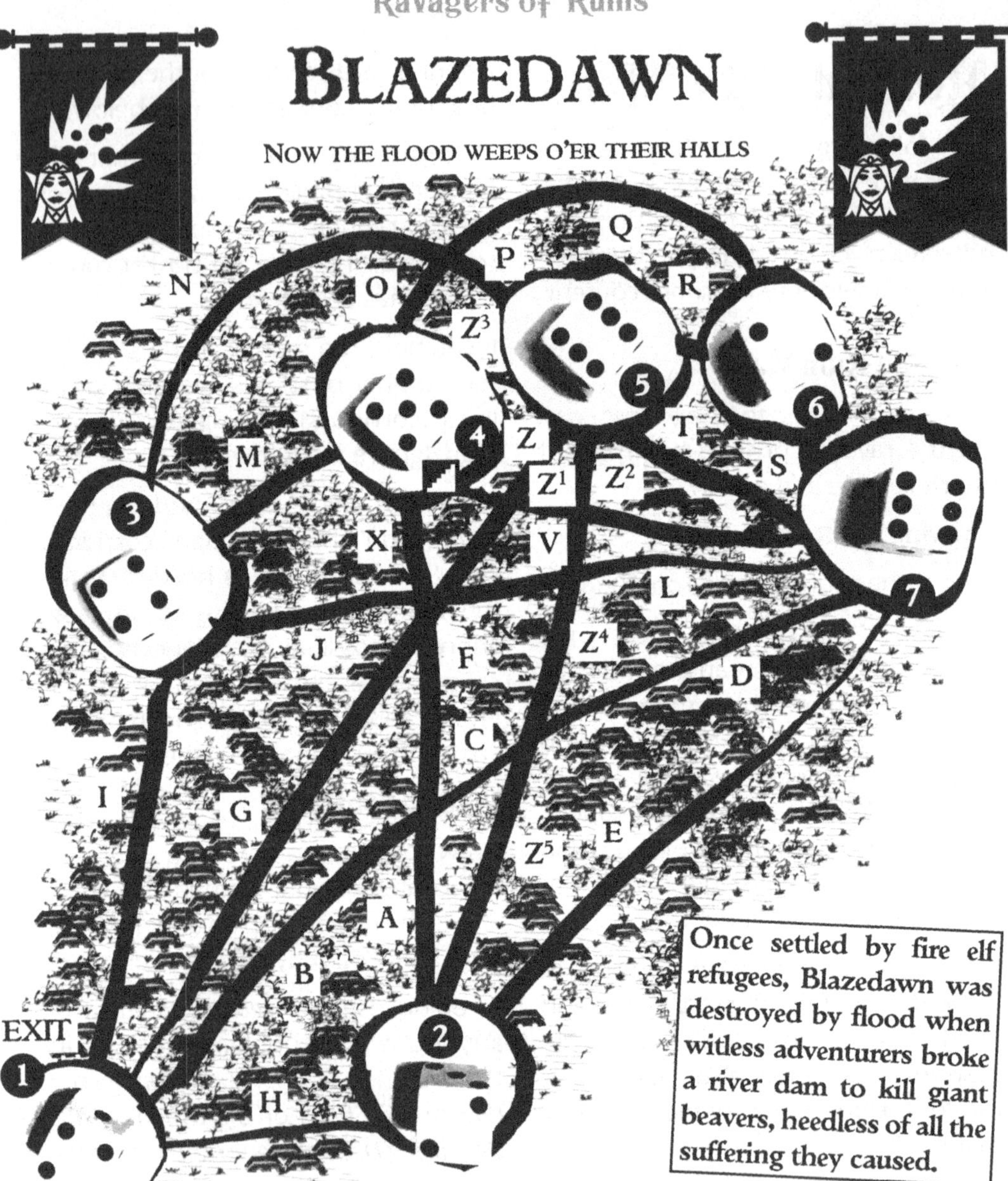

The tangled mess of Blazedawn's ruins were generated with the Ruined City rules. Some of the dice fell off the map, so that it has only seven areas ("rooms") but a lot of crisscrossing corridors (31), since the dice rolls were high. Each line is a corridor; their intersections mark the beginning of a corridor and the end of another. Most areas lead to one another, but some paths will involve more encounter rolls. For example, you could move from Room 1 to Room 7 through corridors B+C+D or H+A+C+D or H+Z5+D, etc. H+E is shortest, but involves going through Room 2. Remember that you must exit the dungeon; pick the safest path as you return!

Leaving and Returning

Once you leave the ruins, the adventure is over. Normally, you can't return to a dungeon you left except under specific circumstances, such as rescue missions for petrified comrades (see 4AD). If you decide to return anyway, roll again for random content in all the rooms and corridors you explored. Traps will have been re-armed under the Trapsmaker Guild warranty. Only permanent features, such as Special Features, will remain.

Ruined City Tables

Ruined City Treasure table (d6)

1. **Trash:** dirt, pebbles and dried excrement (2d6 handfuls).
2. **Trinkets:** worth 3d6 gp.
3. **Gear:** choose any single non-magical piece of equipment worth 50 gp or less.
4. **Wine Bottles:** worth 2d6 x 10 gp.
5. **Old Papers:** get d2 clues or 100 gp.
6. **Magic Ring:** Roll on the Ruined City Magic Rings table.

Ruined City Minions & Vermin table (d66)

11-13	Blood Brood
14-15	Breaking Ones
16-22	Feasters Below
23	Gargoivods
24-26	Gnoblyns
31-33	Gobbleflings
34	Griefworms
35-36	Implings
41-43	Lampreliads
44	Peregrine Kings
45-46	Reptalids
51-52	Sodality of Xichtul
53-54	Sunhounds
55-61	Thornlasses
62-66	Wormongers

Ruined City Weird Monsters & Bosses table (d66)

11	Arachnecros
12	Brain Boiler
13-15	Clockman
16	Cyclooth
21	Duskdrake
22-23	Dwarven Justiciar
24	Evermourner
25-31	Gunklord
32	Gutter Troll
33-35	Mimicking Beast
36	Nether Medusa
41-42	Ogroll
43-44	Platinum Court
45-46	Quadriloch
51-53	Ratwere
54-56	Satogre
61-62	Soulgazer
63	Swordshade
64-65	Watcher
66	Yule Hag

Why the City Was Destroyed Hearsay subtable (d6)

Roll here to find out the reason why the city was destroyed. It may be true, or not.

1	"It was invaded!" (d6: 1-3 hostile neighbors, 4-5 monsters, 6 Dorantia's legions).
2	"Those evil fire elves burned it down! The only good elf is a dead elf!"
3	"Commoners dared to riot against their ruler! The fools got what they deserved."
4	"The people dug too greedily and too deep, and the Abyss came out."
5	"The townsfolk, or maybe the ruler, annoyed a Chaos Lord. That'll teach them!"
6	"There was a civil war between humans and those nonhuman scum."

Ruined City Special Locations table (d6)	
1	**Dungeon Entrance:** You find a hatch which leads to an underground dungeon. Filled with rubble, this dungeon, which was once "Undercity" sewers, is unconnected to any other underground dungeon on your map. It is possible to have two dungeon entrances in the same location, but they will be distinct and on different levels. See Drawing Map Ruins.
2	**Gallows:** Hanged corpses are a frightening sight. If you succeed a L4 luck save (halflings add +L), you get 2 clues. If you fail, d6 corpses per character animate as caged skeletons (L2 undead vermin, never check morale, no treasure).
3	**Abandoned Shop:** Amidst the ruined wares you find non-magical items of your choice worth up to 2d6x10 gp. These items are common ones you could find for sale in a casual shop (not chainsaws, guns, spades or holy water). On a d6 roll of 1-2, their owner later reports you (mark 1 THIEF tick).
4	**Stalwart Survivors:** They are wary but willing to talk to characters who don't seem violent. For each character in your party whose Attack bonus is 0 or less, get 1 clue. You may kill them to take their treasure (treat them as d6 L2 vermin); if you do mark 1 MURDERER tick. If you return, they'll have left.
5	**Wine Cellar:** You can either take the intact bottles to sell (for a profit of d6xd6xd6 gp) or drink them to the last (heal d3 life and all Madness but suffer a -1 drunkenness penalty to all rolls for the next d3 encounters). If your party includes swashbucklers or satyrs, this last option always happens unless each one of them succeeds a L4 will save.
6	**Wizard's Library:** Perusing the worn books, you find any one Secret you wish from the 4AD book. It must be spent in this adventure. Don't roll for XP.

What's That Thing At the Back of That Room subtable (d6)	
	Use this subtable to decorate your city ruins.
1	Broken beds, pebbles, broken glass, chalk fragments, torn rag-doll.
2	Ravaged furniture, broken barrels, animal refuse and the smell of urine.
3	Rusted tools, cages and dead animals with disturbing mutations.
4	Smashed wood boxes and large piles of rotting fish heads.
5	Talon marks on all walls, broken wood panels and defiled cabinets.
6	Bloody, mangled corpses of townsfolk slain by something horrible.

Ruined City Encounter table (2d6)

2	*(Corridors)* Treat this area as empty. *(Rooms)* **Unspoiled Shop:** You find non-magical goods up to a value of d3x50 gp (ropes, armor, etc.) excluding unique or advanced technology (e.g. no guns). Leftovers will have been stolen if you return later.
3	*(Corridors)* Treat this area as empty. *(Rooms)* **Moist Granary:** Roll d6 for each character who eats. 1-2 rotten (L4 poison save or lose 1 life, halflings add +L), 3-6 it's good (heal 1 life).
4	**Beggars:** Crippled survivors, they plead for food and alms. You may brutalize them into giving up their goods (mark 1 THIEF tick): they have a random City Ruins treasure hidden nearby on a d6 roll of 5-6. If you offer them food or gold, they will thank you: mark the COMMISERATION keyword.
5	*(Corridors)* Treat this area as empty. *(Rooms):* Roll on the **Ruined City Special Locations** table.
6	*(Corridors)* Treat this area as empty. *(Rooms)* **Unstable Footing:** All party members must succeed a L3 stoneworks or traps save or lose 1 life (rogues and dwarves add +L). This "trap" cannot be disarmed (it's active each time you return here) but a rogue or dwarf in the 1st rank can detect and warn the party on a successful save. Roll for wandering monsters (1 on d6) if all heroes miss their save: 1-4 Ruined City Minions and Vermin, 5-6 Ruined City Weird Monsters and Bosses.
7	**Collapsing Building:** All party members must save vs L4 traps or lose 1 life. Rogues in the 1st rank can disarm the trap as usual.
8-9	Roll on the **Ruined City Minions & Vermin** table.*
10-12	Roll on the **Ruined City Weird Monsters & Bosses** table.*

** Alternatively, when monsters are met draw cards from Pocketlands' Bestiary Deck.*

What Did That Building Use to Be subtable (d6)

Roll on this table to find out what your current room used to be before the disaster came. This has no game effect but may give you ideas.

1	Unrecognizable Ruins (d6): 1-2 collapsed, 3-4 burnt down, 5-6 pile of stones.
2	Houses (d6): 1-3 small, 4-5 big (d3 stories), 6 totally wrecked.
3	Artisan (d6): 1 shoemaker, 2 tailor, 3 jeweler, 4 stonecutter, 5 tanner, 6 smith.
4	Noble mansion (d6): 1 garden, 2 summer house, 3 garçonnière, 4-6 manse.
5	Pleasure Establishment (d6): 1-2 tavern, 3-4 gambling den, 6 cathouse.
6	Food Shop (d6): 1 butcher, 2 fishmonger, 3 winemaker, 4 bakery, 5 mill, 6 farm.

Ruined City Magic Rings table (d6)	
Unused rings sell for 100 gp. Spent rings sell for 4d6 gp.	
1	**1 Healing Ring:** One use. The ring heals all of its bearer's life and cures all disease and conditions (like a Blessing spell).
2	**Ring of Elfishness:** One use. Your party may envelop themselves in it to ignore one encounter, stepping back whence they came. If you return to that location later, the encounter will still happen.
3	**Ring of the Shrieker:** One use. Kiss the ring to summon a large wading bird with pale red feathers, whose enchanted shriek will cause a single group of minions or vermin to flee immediately.
4	**Ring of Schadenfreude:** Crafted by the Murdermages of the Chrysalis College of Chastity, those who wear them are immune to all forms of charm, mesmerizing, hypnosis, mind control or seduction. Moreover, each time another character loses life during the course of wooing, the ring bearer heals 1 life. The ring loses all power, turning to dust, if removed.
5	**Ring of the Ravening One.** One use. This rings summons a hungry little boy in rags. With supernatural speed and ferocity, the boy sets about eating a target Boss or Weird Monster of your choice, slaying it in a most disturbing way. The boy won't eat Final Bosses, monsters above L6 or deities, who "taste bad". Unless you give the boy food (such as halfling snacks or 1 Food ration), he bites a random character (lose 1 life) as he departs.
6	**Ring of the Ubiquitous One.** One use. This ring summons the spirit of a dead nobleman slain by orcs. He gives you a quest: to find his three missing rings of office. Treat each ring as a distinct "Bring Me Quest" (4AD): you get only one reward if you find them all, but you may choose it instead of rolling on the Epic Rewards table (see 4AD).

What Does That Ring Look Like subtable (d6)	
1	Plain platinum ring with d3 pearls.
2	Bird-shaped ring with conspicuous rubellite adornments.
3	Entwined silver branches with yellow alexandrite.
4	Twin gold bands with white opals (d6) forming a deity's symbol.
5	Thick silver band with golden topaz inscribed with a sad message.
6	Skull-shaped gold studs with tiny sapphire eyes and the glyph of Zur.

Blood Brood

d6+3 Blood Brood. Level 4 Vermin, treasure -2.

Once wounded, the blood brood's targets keep on losing 1 more life on the monsters' turn until a Blessing is cast or, after combat, a bandage is applied. Multiple bites are not cumulative.

Characters who lose over half their maximum life to the blood brood must save vs. L6 curse (clerics add +L, other religious classes add +½L) or they will become minor vampires should they later die, from any cause (see 4AA). Any character they kill always become a minor vampire. Retainers and pets contaminated become blood zombies instead (L3 undead minions, no treasure). Blood dames and the unliving are immune.

Wizards and alchemists can grind them into ghost food (4d6 gp, 4AA).

Reaction: always fight.

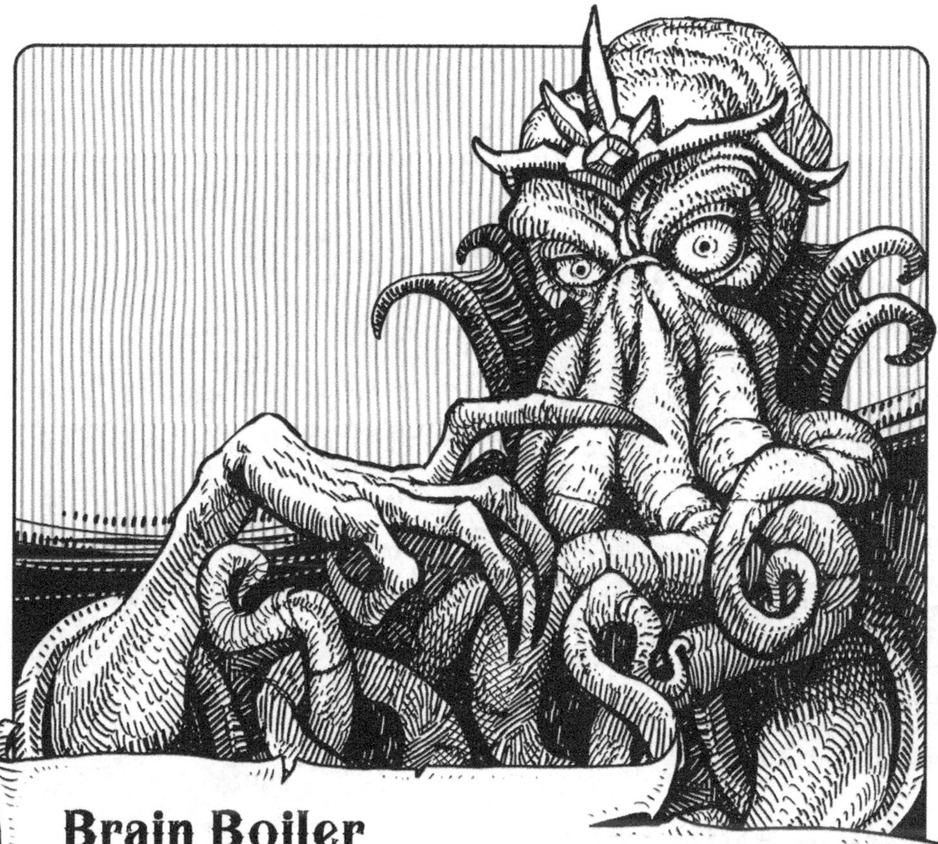

Brain Boiler

Brain Boiler. Level 5 Boss, life 5, morale +1, 3 attacks, treasure +1. Each attack drains 1 spell from the target's memory or d3 chi/psi. Drained spells count as spent. Its attacks always target, in order: 1) Knights of Neutrality, 2) lewd foes (e.g. strumpets), 3) agents of chaos (e.g. clerics), 4) entertainers (e.g. harlequins). It won't attack Law clerics unless struck first. Brain Boilers maintain the Psionic Pylons' gestalt that keeps at bay the cosmic horrors in the Stygian Depths. Alas, strong emotions disrupt the gestalt. The Boiler's quest is always to slay 10 emotion-inducing NPCs: strumpets, entertainers, wizards, chaos monsters, chi users. While their goals converge with the Inquisition's, the latter abhor all nonhumans and ironically fight all Boilers they find. Their reward is either 5 gp per foe slain or a random magic item.

Wizards and alchemists can use their brains like psyker's arachne (TCOTFD).

Reactions: "fight" (if any if quest targets are present) otherwise "quest".

Breaking One

Endless corpses pile up in the Undercity sewers and catacombs, the result of politics and wickedness, prime material for necromancers. But few of the walking dead are as frustratingly relentless as the Breaking Ones.

Breaking Ones (d6+2). Level 3 undead minions, never check morale, treasure -1. Slashing weapons attack them at -1.

Roll d6 for each one slain. On a 1-2, it is not destroyed but shatters, its remnants splitting into two Breaking Ones, each with this splitting ability.

Casting a Blessing might prevent a band of Breaking Ones from splitting. If cast by a cleric who worships a god of Death, this is automatic. Others must win a spellcasting roll equal to the Breaking One's current numbers (clerics add +L). Clerics of Life or Light must double this number.

Reaction (d6): 1-2 peaceful (they are waiting for... something), 3-6 fight.

Clockman

Clockman. Level 5 Weird Monster (automaton), 4 life, 2 attacks, never checks morale, treasure: d6 tech bits (worth 20 gp or 1 Gadget point from W&A). Immune to Sleep, mind spells & poison.

The clockman's powered blades ignore shields. Roll d4 at the end of each of the clockman's turns. If the roll is under the turn's number, it explodes. When the clockman explodes, every party member who fails to save vs. L5 dragon breath (rogues and fire elves add +L) suffers d6 wounds. Each wound point can be substituted by sacrificing instead an item carried (not coins or items without a gp cost).

Reactions (d6): 1-2 inactive (peaceful), 3-6 fight to the death.

Cyclooth

When the world was young, ogres fed from the slaughtered titans, then slept. Large as buildings, the sleeping spawn of Gro Khair now awaken. Hungry.

Cyclooth. Weird Monster, level 4, life 7, 1 attack, morale +1, treasure +2. The Cyclooth's massive but clumsy swings cause 2 damage per hit to a random target. If the Cyclooth fails to hit, it's so angry that its target's Defense is lowered by the Cyclooth's damage on the next turn. If it hits, it doesn't strike the next turn, but drools.

The Cyclooth's awing stupidity radiates around him, causing a -2 penalty to all spellcasting and intelligence-based rolls (like green troll stupidity). After the fight, roll 2d6 for every book or scroll. On a double 1, the scroll or book is erased. Clues from Books that count as Clues will be lost if the books are erased.

Reactions (d6): 1-2 drools (peaceful), 3 fight, 4-6 fight to the death.

Duskdrake

Duskdrake. Level 6 undead Boss, life 5, 1 attack per party member, morale +1, 3 treasures +1. Necromantic spells count as Lightning Bolts vs. them. Duskdrakes are spectral dragons that can summon the souls of the malcontent dead, those fallen because of their comrades' treachery or incompetence. At the start of each of its turns, one former party member now dead returns to fight the party as a Boss (character) or minion (retainer) at their former L+3. Roll d6 if multiple candidates apply (1-3 character, 4-6 retainer), up to your number of dead allies. They keep the same life and number of attacks they had but no other ability. If you don't remember, up to d6 retainers (L3 minions) and d3 characters (L5 Bosses, 5 life, 1 attack, no treasure) will be reanimated.

Reactions (d6): 1-2 quest, 3-4 bribe (all your gold), 5-6 fight.

Dwarven Justiciar

This dwarven champion is devoted to settle all the wrongs committed against his people, recorded in his Scroll of Vengeance. He forgets or forgives nothing.

Justiciar. Level 5 Boss, life 6, never checks morale, treasure +1. Immune to Sleep and mind-affecting spells. His blows cause ½ the target's L in wounds, rounded down. If your party ever killed dwarves, the Justiciar and his retinue of 2d6 dwarf expurgators (L4 minions, morale +1) will fight to the death. If you don't remember, he thinks you did! If the Justiciar was met in a room, there is always a bloodied altar of Tamas Zeya. If you sanctify the altar with the heads of 6 different nonhuman humanoids, the deity will grant your party an Epic Reward.

Reactions (d6): 1-2 quest (always "Being me his head!"; 3-6 fight.

Evermourner

The angels of Peace shed a tear for every wicked act. You can't slay them. Legend says the gods send them to Norindaal as a jest, to mock their crying.

Tally, for the current day, your party's kind deeds (**Kindness**): the number of monsters or NPCs bribed, fed, healed or rescued without reward and similar deeds. Also tally your vile deeds this day (**Vileness**): the number encounters where you attacked first, of NPCs you stole from or enslaved, of THIEF and MURDERER ticks. For every point by which Vileness exceeds Kindness, all party members must succeed a L4 swimming save as the angel's tears drown the area or lose 1 life (max 4 rolls per character). If your Kindness exceeds Vileness, the angel offers you a random magic item that cannot cause loss of life (e.g. re-roll weapons and Fireball wands). If you don't remember your party's deeds, assume your Kindness is 0 and your Vileness d6.

Feaster Below

Extreme poverty bring the destitute to feast on carrion and corpses, slowly degenerating into mindlessness. The worst danger is becoming like them.

Feasters Below (2d6). Level 3 vermin, morale -1, treasure -1. For each one of them killed, another one won't attack next turn but eat its corpse instead during the monsters' turn. After combat, those bitten by Feasters must save vs. a curse (L is equal to the number of life lost during that combat). Those who fail become Feasters and flee. A Blessing can cure this curse if the caster wins a spellcasting roll against the character's L+2. Clerics and wizards add +L to the roll.

Reactions (d6): 1-3 offer food and drink (get 1 Madness if you do eat... that, fight if you refuse), 4 flee, 5-6 flee if outnumbered.*

* Characters whose Madness exceeds their L become feasters.

Gargoivod

The amnesiac gargoivods are animated by the harrowed souls of apprentices who failed the ordeals of the Sphylix School of Sorcery's Magic Tower.

Gargoivods (d3+1). Level 5 minion (construct), never check morale, treasure +1. Immune to Sleep, Illusion, Song of Charm and other mind spells. Surprise on d6 rolls of 1-5. Slashing weapons can't harm them. Gargoivods are only dispatched to guard secret libraries; you get +1 to Search rolls in their lair when it is cleared.

Reactions (d6): 1-2 peaceful, 3-6 puzzle (a coded password; level 4).

Gnoblyn

Nasty & cowardly, these half-breeds of gnomes and goblins got the worst of both their kin. These trapsmiths' addiction to games is their sweet spot.

Gnoblyns. Level 4 Boss (horde), life d6+2, treasure +1.

Before you can attack you must face a random trap (see 4AD).

Roll d6 when the gnoblyns are defeated:

1-3 Shredded Boots: All now save at -1 vs traps 'till you buy boots (1 gp).

4-6 Siren: Your next wandering monster roll is always a 1.

7+ Toothgrim's Trap: L5 traps save for all or lose 1 life.

Reactions (d6): 1 flee, 2-3 flee if outnumbered, 4-5 puzzle (L5), 6 bribe (your biggest item).

Gobblefling

Of goblins and halflings born, they are quick, deceitful kleptomaniacs.

d6+2 Gobbleflings. Level 3 minions, treasure -1. 2/6 odds of surprise.

Roll a d3 once before combat for this gang's special abilities:

1) At the start of their 3rd turn, all surviving gobbleflings flee and raise the alarm. The next minions you meet will be at maximum numbers.

2) The gobbleflings' taunts are insufferable. They attack first, and any enemy can only slay a single gobblefling per round, except with spells.

3) Each successful hit by a gobblefling causes no wound, but instead the git runs away with a random item from its target (not armor).

Reactions (d6): 1 flee, 2-3 tell lies (lose 1 clue), 4-6 pickpocket (see #3 above).

Griefworm

The dwarves say that their kindred live on the sun, ruled by quarreling Lava Queens under the unsmiling gaze of the god Luura. They also say that the most prideful of them all, Lavra, was so lovelorn when her husband, the Fire Lord, forsook her for the goddess Elidra, that she vowed all would share her grief. And so did the griefworms come to be.

Griefworms (d6). Level 3 vermin, treasure -2. Foes hit by a griefworm suffer no wound but must succeed a L4 love save or lose 10 gp. Griefworms hate characters in love with someone (you may decide if this applies to your party).

Reaction: always fight.

Grelflin

Mixed-bloods of gremlin and elf, pickpockets throughout. Grelflins are fascinated by letters and books, and – oddly – prove to be wise scholars.

Grelflins (2d6). Level 2 minions, normal treasure.

Offering the grelflins a book (any) makes them friendly ("peaceful").

Each turn, d3 more grelflins join the fight until all are slain or flee.

If you flee, each party member loses d3 items of your choice which include a random letter (pick a Scrabble letter or roll 4d6: 4=D, 5=E, etc.)

Reactions (d6): 1 quest, 2 flee, 3 puzzle (lose items if you fail, as above), 4-5 pickpocket (distribute grelflins among the party then make one L3 pickpocket save for each, losers lose 1 item/grelflin as above), 6 fight.

Gunklord

Myth says It Who Lies Below played first in the Godgame, creating fungi and slimes. It was trumped when dragons and humanoids ravaged the world, forcing the bitter deity to shelter its servants underground. Over aeons, the oldest fungi folk have been merging into Gunklords, ready for the revolution.

Gunklord. Level 4 Boss, 6 life, d3 attacks (roll each turn).

d6 fungi folk (L3 minions, see 4AD) guard the Gunklord at all times and must be defeated before you can attack it.

Crushing weapons hit the boneless gunklord at -1. When the sewer sovereign's life gets under 4, it explodes in gooey chunks, creating 1 fungi folk (L3 minion, see 4AD) per life point it started with.

Reactions (d6): 1-2 quest, 3 puzzle (L5), 4-6 fight.

Gutter Troll

When they get too old, town trolls turn feral. These gutter trolls grow to enormous size, overwhelmed by ravenous hunger, and become unkillable.

Gutter Troll. Level 5 Boss, 5 life, 2 attacks, 4 treasures.

When a failed Defense roll's result is over the character's current life, the gutter troll bites for d3 wounds instead of 1. Even worse, they regenerate 1 life per turn, even from fire, acid and magic. Crushing weapons don't harm them. The only way for a gutter troll to "die" is, when its life is at 0, for 3 party members to make an attack action to hack away its head and both its arms, and then carry the irate bits in both hands until they can be locked away in separate chests.

Defeating a gutter troll is worth 1 additional XP roll.

Reaction (d6): Spew acid (all lose 1 life, then fight), 2-3 fight, 4-6 fight to the death.

Implings

Vigilant watchers with eagle eyes and obedient to a fault, implings – selectively bred from imps and halflings – work for the watch in several towns to identify and report criminals from their rooftop eyries.

Perched above rooftops, implings are always watching and will report all crimes that happen where you met them. They won't help though.

2d6 Implings. Level 2 vermin, morale -1, treasure: d6 gp each. Only party members with ranged weapons, spells or flight may harm them. When forced to fight, implings will direct all their attacks against the character with the lowest Defense bonus. Defeated foes are captured. Killing an impling patrol causes 1 MURDERER tick if any escape.

Reaction: fight if you have any MURDERER ticks, otherwise peaceful.

Lampreliad

Creeper-like lampreys, these pests abound in unclean, festering towns. Gossip attributes their creation to the wizard Woethong's dangerous dabbling.

Lampreliads (d6+1). Level 3 vermin (plant), treasure -2, never check morale. Immune to Sleep, illusions and all mind-based spells.

Any plant-related spell, like many Blossom spells and Druid spells, works as a Sleep spell against the lampreliads. Lampreliads can't attack fleeing heroes but steal 1 random object they aren't wearing or carrying in hand. The smell of goblin blood excites lampreliads. If your party killed goblins or goblin-kin (e.g. gobbleflings, Grelflins) on this same day, increase the lampreliad colony's level by 1. The same goes for wounded goblins.

Lampreliads never attack plant characters (e.g. treefolk, flower demons).

Reaction: always fight.

Mimicking Beast

Morphing into any furniture, these nasty things spread like a plague.

The Book of Skalitos' putatively spurious claim that Mimicking Beasts are born from the mating of high elves and furniture brought the irate ambassador from Elidren at the Sphylix school to offer a 1,000 gp bounty for the old fool's head.

Mimicking Beast. Level 4 Weird Monster, life: ¼ party's current life (round up), 1 attack per foe, treasure +3. These evolved relatives of the chest monster surprise on a d6 roll of 1-5. Their only weakness is their irresistible fondness for puzzles.

Reactions (d6): 1 peaceful, 2-4 puzzle (level d3+3), 5-6 fight.

Nether Medusa

Demonic cousins of their common kin, they fled from Hell for a better life.

Nether Medusa. Level 4 Weird Monster, 3 life, 2 attacks, 2 treasures. Upon meeting the nether medusa, a L5 gaze save must be made otherwise the target is petrified (see 4AD). Add the target's rank in the marching order as a bonus (heroes in the front rank save at +1, heroes in the rear rank save at +2). The medusas' melee attacks are poisoned snake bites (L3 poison save or lose 1 level till blessed. A target reaching L0 is turned to stone).

The lonely medusa is eager to play games. Alas, she can't withhold her stone gaze if you undertake her puzzle, so your party must still save.

Reactions (d6): 1-2 quest, 3-5 puzzle (but see above), 6 fight.

Ogroll

The offspring of trolls and ogres, the witty ogrolls are oft trusted lieutenants of chaos lords, Viscounts or mob enforcers. They love chess.

Ogroll. Level 5 Boss, 6 life, treasure +1. Each hit causes 2 wounds. Ogrolls regenerate 1 life at the beginning of their turn, even after death, unless killed by fire, acid or a spell, or should a character use one attack to chop an already killed ogroll to bits.

Ogrolls always lead 2d6 underlings of motley species (L3 minions, morale +1 as long as the ogroll lives). Make a morale check for them should the ogroll flee or die.

Reactions (d6): 1 quest, 2-4 puzzle, 5-6 fight.

Platinum Court

It is whispered that the Harrowing Hierophant, Grand Master of the Chaos Lords, extends velvet invitations for guests to commit atrocious acts, for unfathomable purposes. These invitations are not to be refused. Should his quest not be completed within the next day, the Platinum Court will return at midnight to claim the offenders' souls. Even Viscount Visfafen of Almyrli dared not refuse when his turn came...

The Platinum Court. Level 4 undead Boss (Horde), life 6, never check morale, 1 Attack per foe, treasure +1. Every jewel and gem the party carries burns like hellfire in the Court's presence, causing their carrier 1 wound each on the Court's first turn unless a L4 magic save succeeds. Clerics of Zur, Turn Undead and anti-undead magic have no power over them.

Reactions (d6): 1-2 quest, 3-6 fight.*

** If you meet them again without the quest complete, they fight to the death.*

Quadriloch

Quadriloch. Level 5 Weird Monster, 6 life, 3 attacks, 2 treasures +1. Quadrilochs hide in towns, posing as beautiful, normal people. They just want to be loved. All characters (not retainers or pets) must FAIL a L8 magic save upon meeting a quadriloch the first time (wizards add +L). If any save succeeds, the illusion breaks and the fiend attacks.

If all saves fail, the quadriloch appears as an attractive member of the town's dominant ethnicity. In that case, their reaction is "offer food and rest". Should any Blessing or anti-illusion spell be used in their presence (e.g. using the Dispel Illusion spell), they revert forcibly to their true shape and attack, consumed by rage.

Wizards and alchemists can grind a quadriloch heart into Fool's Gold (4AD).

Reaction: see above.

Peregrine King

Forgotten kings, they bide their time, hiding their heirlooms in sewers.

Peregrine Kings (d3+1). Level 5 minions, treasure +2.

Peregrine kings see themselves as royalty and expect servile demonstrations of deference. If a single character succeeds a L5 humility save or offers a gem worth at least 10 gp, they will agree to transport the party anywhere (once, no return), using teleportation. Otherwise, they fight. They accept surrenders that come with a 20 gp bribe. Peregrine kings who flee teleport away with their treasure.

When fighting peregrine kings, keep track of all Attack rolls: if the next Attack roll isn't at least as high as the previous one, the Attack misses as the bird kings blink aside. Death awaits in prolonged fights.

Reaction: expect genuflection (see above).

Ratwere

When rats breed a 7th ratling for 7 generations in a row, it's a ratwere.

Ratwere. Level 4 Boss (Chaos), 4 life, morale -1, 2 treasures. Immune to Sleep. A ratwere's bite destroys a scroll or book. Several rats (3d6 L1 vermin) escort the ratwere at all times.

If the party ever killed rats, they will fight. If you forgot, assume you have. If not, the ratwere demands a bribe of 5d6 gp to buy food for its protégés. There is but a single ratwere in any town, the rat god's guardian for rats. If it dies, another take its place.

Reaction: see above.

Satogre

Love knows no bounds, but the offspring of an ogress and a satyr push awkwardness beyond the boundaries of reason. And they're... simply irresistible.

Satogre. Level 4 Boss, life 4, 2 attacks, treasure +1. If charming, the pheromones of satogres require all humanoid females to save vs. L4 save. Failure results in swooning and coy giggling. They won't fight, flee or do anything else until a day passes, the satogre leaves or he is defeated. If the entire party is swooned, roll d6: 1-3 let's not go into details (consenting ladies of your choice heal 3 life), 4-6 the party gives the satogre all its jewels and gems. In combat, satogres cause 2 wounds with their horns.

Characters who resist the satogre's charm must save vs. L5 philosophy (clerics add +L, all spellcasters add +½ L), as he's delighted to have an intelligent conversation (for once). Those who save get 1 clue. If all fail, he angrily attacks first.

Reactions (d6): 1-2 charm/philosophical discourse (see above), 5-6 fight.

Sodality of Xichtul

Town denizens give a wide berth to the four-armed mummies that stalk the Undercity and even, at night, the most disreputable streets. Clerics say that the Sodality of Xichtul seeks the souls of wizards to expand their master's spy network, for all that their eye-medallions see, the Harrowing Hierophant sees too from his Black Pyramid in An Nur, whence he leads the Chaos legions.

d6 Sodality of Xichtul. L6 minions (chaos undead), never check morale, treasure +2. Instead of attacking, each turn they project horrid visions, causing their targets to spend their next turn harming themselves (either gain 1 wound or 1 Madness and lose the next action) unless they succeed a save vs. the Sodality's numbers. Pulling one's eyes out immunizes to this. After defeating a spellcaster, the Sodality leaves. Arcane Tanners can make a Parchment of Banishing with them (4AA).

Reactions (d6): 1-2 peaceful (they seek someone else), 3-6 fight.

Soulgazer

Soulgazer. Level 4 Weird Monster, 5 life, 3 attacks, treasure +1. Add the party's Madness, Melancholy and Neurosis to its life.

This cruel, playful abomination consumes souls. Before combat, roll d3 for the soulgazer's power on the list below. When it kills a party member, it gains a new one. If you roll a power it already possesses, increase its L by 1 instead.

1) Each time a party member loses 1 life, the soulgazer heals 1 life.

2) Party members cannot heal until the fight is over.

3) Metal weapons and mind spells (e.g. Sleep) cannot harm it.

Soulgazers shun light: lantern bearers defend at +2, but it hates them. Those killed by soulgazers cannot be resurrected nor soul burned.

Reaction: always puzzle (L6).

Sunhound

Thickset humanoids with dark orange fur and luminous unblinking eyes, scholars argue whether sunhounds are Luura's brood or the pets of the sun queen Scoria, kin of hellhounds and fire elves. Every seven years, their martial hordes sail from the sun on golden sky-ships to assail Norindaal cities for jewels. The cruelest ones stay long after, to play.

Sunhounds (d6). Level 5 minions, morale +1, treasure +1 (replace scrolls by gems). Every odd turn, all present must save vs. L3 dragon breath or lose 1 life (all scrolls and books carried are destroyed on a roll of 1). You must leave the map if any sunhound survives after the 7th turn as the entire ruined city is ablaze, ending your adventure.

Reactions (d6): 1 quest (bring 50 gp in gems), 2 puzzle, 3-4 bribe (10 gp each in gems), 5-6 fight.

Swordshade

Legend says that the smith god Darim crafted the first demon sword from a slain demon's remains as a gift for Zur, deity of death, to cleanse its demesne from the invading Blasphemous Ones. What is certain is that demonic weapons who gorge on too many souls develop a wicked sentience of their own, manifesting chaotic ectoplasmic forms to sate their ravenous lust for mortal souls.

Swordshade. Level 5 Weird Monster (artificial construct), 3 life, 3 attacks, morale +1, treasure +1. Immune to Sleep. Party members suffer a penalty to Attack rolls equal to their rank in the marching order (heroes in the front attack at -1, heroes in the rear attack at -2). Foes slain by a swordshade cannot be resurrected as their soul is lost to nightmarish realms.

Reaction: always fight.

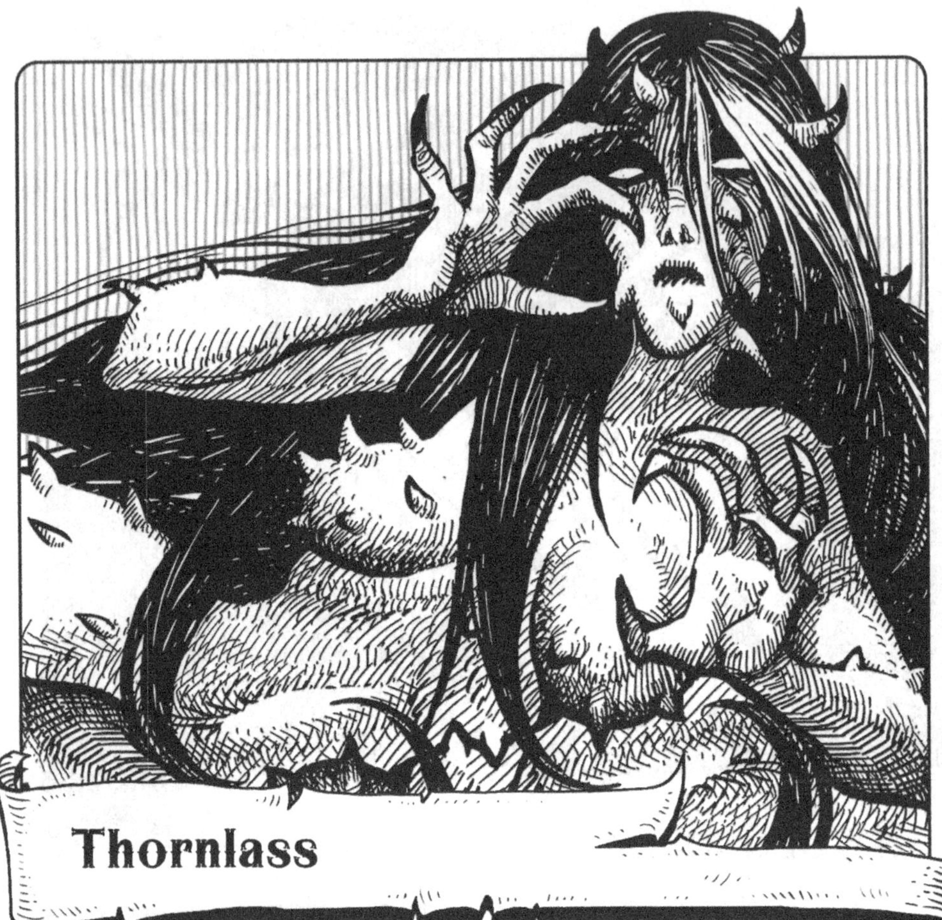

Thornlass

Thornlasses, also known as the Damsels of Thorns, were once the fairest daughters of the Blue-Haired Queen but jealous Elidra, goddess of beauty and song, cursed them. Lovelorn, thornlasses seek the embrace of love, yet their poisoned thorns harm their oft unwilling lovers.

d6+2 Thornlasses. Level 3 minions (flower demons), treasure +1. Those "hit" by their longing touch must save vs. L3 magic or sleep until the next mission. A Blessing cures this affliction.

Option: Should a man immune to poison succeed at wooing these maidens (see TCOTFD), they fall in love and give him their treasure.

Reaction: always supplicate for comforting embrace (counts as "fight").

Watcher

It's been watching you through mirrors for a long time. Delighted, perverse.

Watcher. Level 5 Weird Monster, life 5, 2 attacks, treasure +2.

Watchers are voyeurs that can see through any reflective surface, even water. They know what you did and delight in whispering your misdeeds for all to hear as you near their lair. Before the encounter, all sentient retainers (not pets) must check morale or flee if they fail. At the start of its 2nd turn, the Watcher reanimates the last minion group or Boss you killed and you must fight it again as the Watcher waits yonder.

Ranged weapons and spells strike the flying Watcher at +1.

Reactions (d6): 1 quest, 2 peaceful, 3-5 fight.

Wormonger

d3+1 Wormongers. Level 4 demon minions, morale +1, 2 treasures. Targets hit by their maws' toxic saliva must save vs. L3 poison or be paralyzed (artificials and undead are immune, demons and alchemists save at +1). A Blessing lifts the paralysis.

Paralyzed captives are bound to their palpitating eggs by parasitic umbilical cords. The hatchlings will eventually consume them even as the cords bring ecstatic visions. Severing the cord will cause d3 wounds and 1 permanent Madness to the captive. Captives whose Madness exceeds their L lose their minds (remove them from your party). Wizards, alchemists and beastmasters can make d3+1 healing potions from these eggs.

Reaction: always fight.

Yule Hag

Yule Hag. Level 4 Boss (angel of Peace/Triad), life: 1/20 the party's total carried wealth in gp (min. 1, max 20), morale +3, no treasure. Immune to Sleep and mind spells. She protects the poor. If the party ever killed a beggar, she fights. If not, and you have the COMMISERATION keyword, the Yule Hag heals d3 life to all. Otherwise – even if attacked – each character must succeed a wealth save against 1/10 their wealth in gp (counting gold, gems, jewels but not bank deposits, magic items or gear). The witch can be given wealth before the save (it disappears). You can't reallocate items, drop them or cheat. Those who fail lose 1 gp in wealth per point of failure. Giving all carried wealth to the hag earns 1 XP. Her hits cause 1 wound per 100 gp of wealth her target carries (round down). Virgins, retainers and beasts can't cause her wounds, whatever they do.

Reaction: see above. She never kills, leaving when her foes have but 1 life.

You never know where your party is going to travel next. Whether you're preparing for a campaign or mapping the adventure as it unfolds, geomorph cards help you create attractive maps in no time. Make a Never-Ending game world map! Be open, be creative, and be spontaneous, for your character and as a group!

EACH SET FEATURES:

- Detailed color minimap cards
- Standard poker size
- 5 x 5 grid with iconic terrain
- The maps work cohesively with each other

WWW. POCKETLANDS .COM

Made in the USA
Middletown, DE
27 July 2024